*The Cat Who
Wanted to go Home*

Jill Tomlinson

Suzy is a little striped cat who lives in a French seaside village with a fisherman and his four sons. She loves Gaby, the youngest, the most because he strokes her fur the wrong way. Ever inquisitive, she climbs into the basket of a balloon one day, and gets carried off over the Channel to an English seaside village. But Suzy makes many daring attempts to get back home . . .

Jill Tomlinson

The Cat Who
Wanted To Go Home

Illustrated by Joanne Cole

A Magnet Book

Also by Jill Tomlinson

THE OWL WHO WAS AFRAID OF THE DARK
PENGUIN'S PROGRESS
THE AARDVARK WHO WASN'T SURE
THE HEN WHO WOULDN'T GIVE UP
THE GORILLA WHO WANTED TO GROW UP
THE OTTER WHO WANTED TO KNOW

First published in Great Britain 1972
by Methuen Children's Books Ltd
Methuen Paperback edition
first published 1978
by Methuen Children's Books Ltd
11 New Fetter Lane, London EC4P 4EE
Magnet edition published 1979
Text copyright © 1972 Jill Tomlinson
Illustrations copyright © 1972
Methuen Children's Books Ltd
Cover artwork copyright © 1978
Methuen Children's Books Ltd
Reproduced, printed and bound
in Great Britain by Cox & Wyman Ltd, Reading

ISBN 0 416 86550 X

Contents

For Tricia
and her children,
Joanna, Roderick and Caroline,
not forgetting
D.H.

1 An unusual basket

Suzy was a little striped cat. She had stiffly starched white whiskers and a fine pair of football socks on her front paws.

Suzy lived in the house of a fisherman in a little seaside village in France. The fisherman had four sons. Pierre was ten years old, Henri was eight, Paul was six and Gaby was four, so when they stood in a row they looked like a set of steps. All the boys played with Suzy and they took her with them everywhere.

Pierre, the eldest one, made Suzy a

scratching-post by wrapping a bit of old carpet round one of the fat legs of the big kitchen table. Suzy could sharpen her claws whenever she liked.

Henri knew which were the best tickly places on her spotted tummy. Although all the rest of her was covered with black stripes, Suzy's tummy was fawn with black spots. Henri said she was a tiger on top and a leopard underneath. Anyway, he was a jolly good tickler.

Paul made a toy for her. He tied a piece of crackly paper to the end of a long piece of string and pulled it along on the ground for her to chase. Suzy could run very fast and Paul could not keep ahead of her for very long. She would pounce and catch the paper again and again. Paul would stand still to get his breath back and dangle the bit of paper just out of reach above her head. Suzy would leap and leap to catch it, with Paul jerking it away when she got too near. Paul was great fun.

But Gaby, the youngest, was the best. Suzy adored him – and for a very odd reason. Gaby didn't know the proper way to stroke a cat. Most cats like being stroked from head to tail, the way the fur lies. But Gaby always stroked Suzy the wrong way – backwards from tail to head – and Suzy *loved* it. She would wriggle against his hand with delight, purring like a sewing machine, asking him to do it again and again. She liked it better than anything in the world. Yes, even better than eating fish. And Suzy liked eating fish very much indeed – which was just as well because she had it for breakfast and supper every day.

The boys always helped their father when he came home in his boat with his catch of fish. Every day they waited for him on the quay – Pierre and Henri and Paul and Gaby and Suzy. She was allowed to eat as much as she wanted of the fish that were too small to be sold. There was always something for Suzy even when the catch wasn't very good. She would have grown fat if the boys had not given her so much exercise.

Suzy hated it when the boys were at school and there was nobody to play with her; nobody to dangle a bit of string or throw a ball or to climb trees with her. She would wander round the quay by herself getting in everybody's way, or go exploring in the fields behind the village.

One day she was chasing butterflies across a field when she nearly bumped into a huge basket. Suzy was used to baskets – there were lots of them on the quay – but this one was much bigger. Suzy climbed up the steep side and peered in. The basket was so big that there was a wooden stool inside. Under the stool was a nice patch of shade.

It was a very hot day. Suzy decided to have a little nap. She jumped lightly down into the basket and settled herself nose to tail under the stool. Curled round like that she looked like a huge furry snail.

Suzy was soon fast asleep.

When she woke up Suzy felt very peculiar.

The basket seemed to be rocking from side to side, joggling her. She rushed to the edge of the basket and climbed up the side to jump out – but she changed her mind when she looked over the top! The ground was a very long way away – much too far for her to jump. She clung on tightly as the basket jerked again, grabbing at a rope with her paws.

Ropes? She had not noticed them when she climbed in. Suzy looked up. The ropes were attached to a huge balloon – an *enormous* balloon. Suzy was floating high up in the sky in a basket suspended from a balloon!

Poor Suzy! She slid back into the basket and crouched on the floor, shivering with fright.

Then she felt a gentle hand on her back and looked up to find that there was a man in the basket with her.

'Hello, little cat,' he said. 'I didn't invite you! Oh well, it's too late now. You will have to come with me to England.'

Suzy didn't know where England was, but she knew she didn't want to go there. She wanted to stay in France in her own little fishing village with the boys.

'Chez-moi!' she wailed. It sounded like 'shay-mwa'. She was saying in French that she wanted to go home.

But the man had to jump up to do something with the balloon, which was swinging wildly, and from then on was too busy to take any notice of his little passenger.

So Suzy floated across the sea between France and England by balloon! She hated every joggly moment of it. The worst part was seeing the coast of France disappear behind them – France and Pierre and Henri and Paul and Gaby, France and everything she knew and loved.

'Chez-moi!' she wailed again, but nobody heard her. There were big puffy clouds sailing underneath them and sometimes what looked like toy ships on the sea far below. It was really very interesting and beautiful, but Suzy could only think about one thing. How was she going to get back across this huge stretch of water?

They landed in England with a bump. Suzy had not realized that they were back over land again because for the last bit she had had her eyes tightly shut. She jumped out of the basket and ran. She could not get away from that balloon fast enough.

Because she was very hungry, she ran towards a fishy smell. But the smell was coming from the sea and there were no fish and no fishing boats. This was an English seaside town and not a bit like her own village. There was just a wide expanse of concrete in front of the sea, with steps down to the sand. Poor Suzy. She sat miserably on the sea-front looking out at the waves. How was she going to get home across all that water?

Luckily an RSPCA lady came along. It was her job to find homes for lost cats. She

picked up
Suzy and
took her to
the house of
a   kind   old
lady   whom   she
knew, called Auntie Jo.
'Do you think you could
look after this little cat for me,
Auntie Jo?' the RSPCA lady said. 'I've never
seen her before. She's not from around here.
She must be lost.'

'Of course she can stay with me,' said
Auntie Jo. 'She'll be company for Biff.'

Biff was Auntie Jo's new budgie who was
just learning to talk.

'Hello, Auntie Jo,' he said in his funny
cracked voice.

Of course, Suzy could not understand

16

English, but she understood the saucer of milk that Auntie Jo put down for her and she lapped up every drop. Then, because she was a polite cat, she said 'thank you' in French: 'Merci!' It was a miaowing sound, 'mare-see'.

'What a funny miaow you have, Pussy cat,' said Auntie Jo.

'Merci,' said Biff.

'Oh, clever Biff,' Auntie Jo said.

'Clever Biff,' said Biff. 'Merci.'

Suzy was made very comfortable on an old chair that night. Auntie Jo stroked her gently and Suzy purred. She purred in French, but purring sounds the same all over the world, whatever country you come from.

But it wasn't like home. She did miss Gaby stroking her the wrong way.

2 Up and down is no good

So Suzy came to live with Auntie Jo and Biff.

Next morning Auntie Jo got out her tricycle to go shopping. It was a great big one with huge wheels and a basket on the front. Auntie Jo felt that she was too old to wobble about on a bicycle any more, and what was good enough for the little girl next door was good enough for her.

When Suzy saw Auntie Jo standing in front of the mirror in the hall, fiercely jabbing a hat pin into her flat straw hat to keep it

anchored to her bun, she guessed that Auntie
Jo was going out.

When Auntie Jo had pedalled a few yards
down the road she suddenly saw a whiskery
face staring at her over the handlebars.

'Chez-moi!' it said.

Auntie Jo swerved violently and stopped.

'Oh, Pussy! You did frighten me. What are
you doing in there? Go home. Shoo!'

Suzy didn't understand.

'Chez-moi!' she wailed again, settling herself more comfortably in the basket.

'Oh, very well, you can come if you want
to,' said Auntie Jo, starting to pedal again.
'But sit still.'

So Suzy rode down to the sea-front in
great style in Auntie Jo's tricycle basket. She
got very excited when she saw the sea. That
sheet of blue water with white lace trim-

mings was all that lay between her and France. Oh, she would soon be home.

The minute Auntie Jo had parked the tricycle by the butcher's shop and disappeared inside, Suzy jumped down from the basket and ran across the road to the beach. There were children everywhere, digging in the sand and running about with buckets of water, just like French children. Suzy dodged nimbly between them and ran down to the water's edge. She had hoped to find a fishing boat like the one belonging to her family, but there didn't seem to be anything like that – only lots of people shouting and splashing in the water. She was so busy staring out to sea, looking for boats, that she hardly noticed the wavelets trickling across the sand and washing over her paws.

'Oh, look! There's a kitten over there,

paddling!' a little girl said to her father, who was sitting in a deckchair reading his paper.

'Kittens don't paddle, Caroline,' he said. 'Cats hate water.'

'Well, this one is paddling,' said Caroline. 'I'm going down to watch her.'

She dropped her spade and ran down to the sea. Suzy had moved along a bit, but she was easy to find because of the trail of paw-prints she left behind her in the sand.

'Pussy!' said Caroline, putting down her hand and stroking Suzy. Suzy trilled and purred and rubbed against the little girl's hand.

'Oh, you are sweet,' she said, picking her up and holding her against her shoulder. 'Come on, I want to show you to Daddy. He doesn't believe that you've been paddling.'

She started back up the beach, but Suzy

suddenly jumped down and tore away across the sand towards some rocks. She had seen something! From Caroline's shoulder she had had a better view over the top of people's heads, and she was sure she had seen a boat. A boat! She could get home at last.

Caroline started to follow her, but Suzy was going much too fast, and anyway her father would be cross if she just disappeared without telling him where she was going. Bother! Now he would never believe that there *had* been a paddling kitten.

Suzy reached the rocks, and looked about her. Yes! There was the boat. It was a very small plastic canoe, but it was all there was so it would have to do. A small boy was paddling it along close to the rocks. Suzy scrambled towards him over the slippery seaweed and fixed him with her great green eyes.

'Chez-moi!' she called hopefully. 'Chez-moi!'

The boy looked up and stared at her in amazement. He had never seen a cat on the beach before.

'What do you want, Puss? Not a ride, surely?'

Suzy answered by taking a firm grip on the seaweed and leaping neatly into the canoe. She curled her tail round her toes and waited patiently. She was on her way home at last.

But of course she was not. People don't cross the Channel in toy canoes. The little boy was only allowed to go up and down in the shallow water close to the shore. After a few minutes of going up and down, up and down, Suzy began to get restless. This was no good. This wouldn't get her home to France.

'Chez-moi!' she wailed. Why didn't the boy understand how important it was to her to get home? 'Chez-moi!'

'Oh, you want to get out now, do you?' he said. 'Right'o, hang on a tick.'

He pulled in towards a flat rock. When Suzy realized that he was taking her back to land she gave up all hope of getting to France on this trip. She got ready to spring.

'Mind your claws!' shouted the little boy suddenly, as he saw her digging them into the plastic canoe. 'You'll puncture us!'

It was too late, and Suzy didn't understand anyway. She sprang out on to the rock, leaving behind four sets of tiny holes from which the air hissed fiercely. Claws are not good for inflated plastic.

The boy sprang out too, pulling the canoe after him.

'That's the last time I give a ride to a cat,' he grumbled, fishing in his pocket for his repair kit.

The canoe slowly collasped and was quite flat by the time Suzy was back by the butcher's shop. Auntie Jo's tricycle wasn't there, but Suzy remembered the way to her house.

'Pussy cat, Pussy cat, where have you been?' said Auntie Jo when Suzy walked in.

'Pussy cat, Pussy cat, where have you been?' Biff repeated in his funny voice. 'Clever Biff.'

'You are a clever Biff,' said Auntie Jo. 'Well, Pussy cat, here is your dinner.' She put down a saucer of liver.

Suzy ate it all up. It wasn't fish, but it was very nice.

'Merci,' she said, cleaning her whiskers.

'You do have a funny miaow,' said Auntie Jo.

'Merci,' Biff said. 'Clever Biff.'

And Suzy purred.

But she did miss Gaby stroking her the wrong way.

3   *They do it for fun*

Next morning Auntie Jo got out her tricycle again. Suzy hopped into the basket. It was very windy and Auntie Jo had to hang on to her hat all the way down to the shops.

As they came round the corner on to the sea-front they were nearly knocked over. The wind was blowing fiercely from the sea. There were huge waves thundering on the beach.

Auntie Jo managed to park by the grocer's. Suzy went to look at the waves. There would be no chance of getting home to France that day.

Or was there? A young man was pushing his way into the waves holding a flat board above his head. He was definitely going out to sea *towards France*!

Suzy ran towards him, but she was too late; he was already a long way out. He was swimming now, pushing the board in front of him.

She watched him sadly. He was going without her. She had so wanted to go home. Suzy threw back her head and wailed:

'Chez-moi!'

But what was this? The young man must have heard her, because he was coming back. He was coming back for her!

Suzy ran to meet him, not caring how wet she got. He jumped off the board as it grounded on the sand, and Suzy jumped on to it. The young man *was* surprised.

'Do you want to come surfing with me?' he asked. 'I thought cats didn't like water!'

'Chez-moi!' Suzy said.

'Okay. Hang on, though. It's kind of wet out there.'

The young man lifted the surf-board with Suzy on it high above his head, and set off through the waves.

Suzy had to work hard at keeping her balance, but she was happy. France at last.

She was not quite so happy when the young man began swimming, pushing the board in front of him, sometimes *through* the waves. But Suzy just closed her eyes and hung on, spitting out the nasty sea water when she got a mouthful.

Suddenly the young man shouted, 'Here comes a beauty!'

He swung the board round, kneeled on it,

29

and then stood up. A huge wave picked them up and hurtled them back toward the beach – to England. Suzy was furious.

'Chez-moi!' she wailed.

'Yes, isn't it marvellous!' shouted the young man. He thought she was enjoying it as much as he was.

There were some more young men with boards on the beach. They were very surprised to see Suzy.

'Whatever have you got there, Bill?' shouted one of them. 'A new member for the club?'

'Yes,' Bill shouted. 'She's terrific. A real swinger. You watch.'

They all set off out to sea. Suzy was very relieved. Of course, he had just come back for the others, that was all. Now they would go to France.

But, of course, they didn't. They went out

to sea and back again several times before
Suzy realized that they were only doing it for
fun!

The surf-riders thought Suzy was wonderful, and when they came out of the sea for
lunch they made a great fuss of her. They
rolled her in a towel to dry her off a bit and
then fed her with a whole tin of sardines.
Fish! Then they played ball with her and
pulled a belt along the sand for her to chase.

Suzy had a lovely time – even if she didn't get home to France.

When she walked into Auntie Jo's house, Biff said:

'Pussy cat, Pussy cat, where have you been?'

'Yes, where have you been?' said Auntie Jo. 'Swimming, by the look of you. There's seaweed on your tail.'

Suzy sat down and washed herself all over. Auntie Jo pulled off the seaweed. Then she put down a saucer of mince.

Suzy ate it all up. It wasn't fish, but it was very good.

'Merci,' she said, cleaning her whiskers.

'You do have a funny miaow,' Auntie Jo said.

And Suzy purred.

But she did miss Gaby stroking her the wrong way.

4   *Catty paddle*

The next morning Auntie Jo got out her tricycle and Suzy hopped into the basket.

'I'm not sure that I should take you with me,' said Auntie Jo. 'You came back in such a horrible mess yesterday.'

'Chez-moi!' Suzy said, wondering why Auntie Jo didn't start.

'Oh, all right,' said Auntie Jo, 'but you behave yourself today.'

She pedalled off towards the shops. The wind had dropped, and when they came round the corner to the sea-front the sea was flat and calm like glass. Suzy was out of the basket before Auntie Jo had finished parking.

'Oh dear, she's off again,' said Auntie Jo, watching Suzy run down towards the sea. 'She is a funny little cat.'

The funny little cat was looking for *boats*. There must be some boats going to France on a nice calm day like this.

There were some pedal boats going up and down, but Suzy was getting wise. She knew that up and down was no good to her. She needed a boat that was going out to sea.

And there was one – a very fast speedboat. It was pulling a young girl along behind it! She was riding on the water on two long thin boards. She was going very fast. A boat like that would get you to France in no time.

34

Suzy ran down to the end of the pier. There was another speedboat getting ready to go, and there was another girl getting ready to be pulled behind.

Suzy watched her. She had hoped that one of the boats would pull *her* behind it, but those long water skis were much too big for her.

Then the girl got hold of a piece of rope that was dangling from the back of the speed-boat. Suzy wouldn't be able to hang on to that either, not with her tiny paws.

There was only one thing for it – she would have to go along with the girl.

Suzy jumped. She landed on the girl's shoulder, very gently, but the girl was not at all pleased.

'Get off!' she cried. 'What on earth . . . ?' She looked down sideways at her shoulder to see what this furry thing was, but she dare not let go of the rope to push it off because they would be starting any second.

'Oh get off!' she said again, trying to shove Suzy with her chin, but Suzy was not going to be pushed off that easily.

Then it was too late. With a great roar, the speedboat burst away from the pier. The girl tightened her grip on the rope and struggled to keep her balance on the skis, with Suzy teetering on her shoulder.

There were lots of people on the pier watching the water skiers, and they all laughed when they saw Suzy.

'A water-skiing cat!' they said. 'Just look at that!'

The water-skiing cat was having great difficulty in staying on. What could she hang on to? The girl had long hair. Suzy managed to get one paw tangled up in it and hung on to that.

'Ow!' cried the poor girl, but there was nothing she could do about it.

Suzy began to enjoy herself. It was very exciting going so fast, and she wasn't really getting wet at all except for a little spray. Oh, this was a lovely way to go home to France.

Then she noticed something. The other boat had turned round and was going back to the pier! Were they going to do the same?

Yes, their speedboat began to swerve. Suzy was so disappointed.

'Chez-moi!' she wailed loudly into the girl's ear.

It was too much for her. She jumped, lost her balance, and a second later she and Suzy were struggling in the water, the speedboat heading back for the pier without them.

Suzy headed for the pier too. She dis-
covered that she could swim! She did a catty
sort of dog-paddle.

Meanwhile, the crew in the boat realized
that they had lost the water-skier and came
back to pick her up.

'What happened to you?' asked the driver
as he helped her into the boat.

'It was that wretched cat!' she said. 'It was
all its fault.'

'What cat?' said the man. 'I can't see any
cat.'

'Oh dear, she must have drowned, the poor little thing!' The water-skier was suddenly contrite. 'I was so busy trying to keep afloat myself I didn't notice what happened to her.'

'I did,' said the other man in the boat. 'She's swimming. Look! She's nearly at the pier already.'

There was Suzy, sodden and dripping, climbing on to the pier. All the people were cheering. The water-skier was so relieved that Suzy wasn't drowned that she forgave her at once.

Suzy dodged all the people and ran home to Auntie Jo.

'Pussy cat, Pussy cat, where have you been?' said Biff.

'You might well ask!' Auntie Jo said. She looked in horror at the soggy Suzy, dripping on her carpet. 'She's in an even worse state than she was yesterday.'

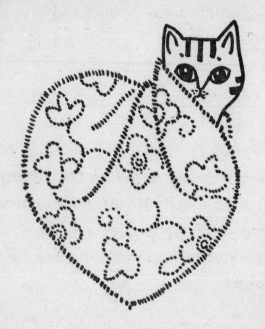

She rubbed Suzy all over hard with a rough towel and put on an electric fire for her to sit by until she was really dry.

Then she gave Suzy her dinner – a saucer of rabbit.

'I'm not sure you deserve it, though,' Auntie Jo said.

Suzy ate it all up. It wasn't fish, but it was very good.

'Merci,' she said, cleaning her whiskers.

Then Auntie Jo gave her a saucer of milk. It was lovely after all that salty water.

'Merci,' she said again.

'You do have a funny miaow,' Auntie Jo said. 'But you're a funny cat altogether.' She stroked her and Suzy purred.

But she did miss Gaby stroking her the wrong way.

5 The wettest way

The next morning Auntie Jo opened her newspaper – and there was a photograph of Suzy water-skiing!

'Well! So that's what you were up to yesterday, Pussy cat!' she said. 'No wonder you were so wet. I think you had better stay at home today.'

But when Auntie Jo wheeled out her tricycle, Suzy popped into the basket as usual.

'Chez-moi!' she said to Auntie Jo, beseeching her with her big green eyes.

'Oh, come on then,' Auntie Jo said.

As they pedalled along the sea-front to the shops, a lady and her husband recognized Suzy.

'Why surely that's the little cat who was water-skiing yesterday,' they said. 'So she belongs to you, does she, Auntie Jo?'

'She's a stray,' Auntie Jo said. 'I'm just feeding her.'

'Well, she's a very good swimmer,' said the lady.

'Yes,' said her husband. 'Let's hope she doesn't get any ideas because of what's happening today.'

'What is happening?' asked Auntie Jo.

'There's a swimmer attempting to cross the Channel. That's a very long way for a small cat.'

'Did you hear that, Pussy cat?' said Auntie Jo. 'No Channel swimming.'

But I'm afraid Suzy didn't understand, and when Auntie Jo parked her tricycle, she popped out of the basket as usual and ran down to the water's edge.

She was looking for boats, of course. There was one small boat and beside it was a great big fat man. It was the Channel swimmer. Somebody was smearing him all over with greasy stuff to keep him warm during his long swim.

Suzy wasn't very interested in all this until she heard somebody say, 'Well, good luck, Jim! Let's hope you get to France.'

France? He was really going to France!

So it was hardly surprising that when the man had been swimming for a few minutes he found that there was a little cat swimming beside him!

The man was swimming very slowly and

steadily because he had a long way to go, but even so it was a bit fast for Suzy, who was having to paddle madly to keep up with him. Clearly she wouldn't be able to do this for very long.

'Go home!' grunted the man.

Suzy didn't understand him, and anyway going home was what she was doing!

'What did you say, Jim?' said his wife, who was going along in the boat to see that he was all right.

'Company,' said Jim. 'Look!'

His wife thought he meant sharks or something.

'Good heavens!' she said. 'Where?'

'Cat,' said Jim.

'Cat?' Jim's wife peered through the waves. Then she saw Suzy.

Suzy was holding her head as high as she

could with her ears folded down to keep out the water. Jim's wife did laugh.

'You look like a mother duck and its baby, Jim,' she said. 'Shall I pick her up?'

'Leave her,' said Jim. 'She's doing fine. I like having her.'

And so Suzy swam the Channel for a bit.

But she began to get very tired and she was afraid of being left behind. The man kept having to wait for her to catch up.

'Maisie, pick her up,' Jim said at last. 'She's slowing me down.'

Suzy felt herself being scooped up out of the water.

'Chez-moi!' she wailed furiously. She ran to the edge of the boat, dived in and started swimming again.

Jim nearly choked. It is very difficult to laugh when you are swimming. Maisie scooped up Suzy once again and this time she trapped her under a lobster pot at the bottom of the boat.

'She seems to be as silly about wanting to swim the Channel as you are!' Maisie said.

Suzy didn't like the lobster pot, but she was so exhausted that she hadn't the energy to fight it for long. She lay down and sulked.

'That's better,' Maisie said. 'You're much too small to swim such a long way. You stay here with me.' She took her out and dried her and wrapped her in a warm towel, keeping a firm hold on her.

It dawned on Suzy at last that the boat was following the swimmer. So she *was* going to France, and really it was much easier to go there on Maisie's lap than by swimming. She settled down happily.

Maisie looked at her watch. 'You're making good time, Jim,' she called out. 'We should catch the tide.'

But she spoke too soon. The wind started to get up and the sea got rougher and rougher. Jim found it more and more difficult to move forward. In the end it got so bad that he was hardly moving at all, and Maisie had to turn off the boat's engine to stay with him. The boat began to be tossed about, too, as the waves got bigger and bigger, and Maisie put Suzy back under the lobster pot to keep her safe.

Jim struggled on for a bit, but it was no good. He would have missed the tide now anyway.

Suzy couldn't believe it when she saw him being helped into the boat, and when the boat turned round and headed back for England it was the last straw.

'Chez-moi!' she cried, heartbroken. 'Chez-moi!'

'I'm sorry, Pussy,' said Jim. 'I thought you were going to bring me luck, but it seems that I was wrong. Never mind. I'll try again tomorrow.'

Suzy only knew that she wasn't going home to France.

'Chez-moi!'

'There, she's telling me she's sorry,' said Jim. He put on a thick sweater and some trousers and had a cup of coffee. Now that the engine was full on, the boat wasn't tossing nearly so much, so Jim took Suzy out of the lobster pot and she rode the rest of the way back to England on his lap. He made a great fuss of her.

'She had plenty of guts, this little one,' he said to Maisie. 'Maybe she couldn't swim the Channel, but I bet she could swim the Thames. I can see it now in *The Guinness Book of Records:* "First cat to swim the Thames in the record-breaking time of five minutes". What about that, Pussy cat?' He stroked Suzy's ears. Suzy purred and then fell fast asleep.

When she woke up they were back at the pier.

'Hard luck, Jim,' people were saying. 'Are you going to try again?'

'Tomorrow if the weather's kind,' he said.

'I think I'll take my lucky cat with me.' He looked around. 'Oh, where is she?'

Suzy had slipped away in the crowd and run home to Auntie Jo.

'Pussy cat, Pussy cat, where have you been?' said Biff.

'Swimming the Channel by the look of her!' Auntie Jo said. 'Oh, Pussy cat, you are a shocker.'

'Shocker!' said Biff. 'Shocker! Clever Biff.'

Auntie Jo dried Suzy again and gave her her dinner – a piece of chicken. Suzy ate it all up. It wasn't fish, but it was very good.

'Merci,' she said, cleaning her whiskers.

'Merci,' said Biff, 'shocker!'

And Suzy purred.

But she did miss Gaby stroking her the wrong way.

6 Suzy nearly goes under

The next morning Suzy waited patiently in the hall by the door while Auntie Jo speared her hat to her bun. It was a different hat today – a flowery one. Auntie Jo saw Suzy reflected in the glass.

'Now, Pussy cat,' she said. 'It's no good you waiting there today. It's Sunday – I'm going to Church. I'm not taking you with me.'

But of course, she was. Suzy settled herself into the basket the minute Auntie Jo had wheeled out her tricycle, and nothing Auntie Jo said or did would move her.

'All right,' said Auntie Jo at last. 'Come – but you'll have to wait outside during the service.'

'Chez-moi!' replied Suzy, quite happy.

Auntie Jo went a different way today, turning out of the town. The Church was at the top of a hill and Auntie Jo had to get off and push the tricycle for the last bit. Suzy didn't mind. She sat up in the basket and looked about her. The church was on a headland – a piece of land which stuck out into the sea – and Suzy could see into the bay on the other side. There were ships there, big ships!

The moment Auntie Jo parked the tricycle by the church porch Suzy was off like a rocket over the headland.

'Oh dear,' said Auntie Jo. 'I hope she doesn't go down to the sea again.'

Suzy took a short cut down a cliff path, streaked across the sand and up some steps to a big quay. There was a smart motor-boat decorated with flags just about to leave the jetty. Suzy jumped neatly down and settled herself behind a pile of rope.

With a roar the motor-boat shot off across the bay, a plume of white foam behind it. There were a lot of men in uniform on board, including an Admiral, but of course Suzy didn't notice that. All she knew was that they were going towards France!

Or were they? The boat was drawing up alongside a very odd sausage-shaped ship. Oh well, perhaps she'd still get there.

Suzy joined the end of the procession that was going aboard the ship. The sailors already on the ship were all lined up ready to be inspected by the Admiral. Someone was making an awful piping noise on a funny kind of whistle.

The Admiral began to strut importantly between the lines of men. Suzy, who was determined not to be left behind, trotted importantly behind him, for all the world as if inspecting the fleet was something she did every day of her life. Eyes front, tail erect, her football-sock paws lifting neatly as she stepped along the deck, Suzy was almost as dignified

as the Admiral himself – and he had all his gold braid to help him!

The men were trying hard not to grin; it was not often that they had to stand to attention to be inspected by a small tabby cat!

By the end of the inspection Suzy was beginning to feel a little impatient. What was all this walking about for? Why didn't they get on with it and make for France?

Well, they did begin to get on with something. The Admiral went back to his motorboat to be taken ashore. Suzy didn't want *that* so she ran and hid behind a sort of tower.

When the Admiral's boat had gone, the ship's Captain gave the order: 'Make ready to submerge!' Of course, Suzy didn't know what that meant.

The sailors rushed about slamming doors and hatches. Suddenly Suzy was the only one left on top of the ship. The men had all disappeared.

Well, as long as she got to France, Suzy didn't mind having a lonely ride.

But what was happening? The ship was sinking! Suzy watched with horror as the ship went down, down and the water came up, up towards her. Soon the main part of the ship had completely disappeared and although Suzy had scrambled to the top of the tower thing, that was sinking too!

Poor Suzy. She clung to the last bit sticking out of the top and stared at the empty sea around her. The shore was terribly far away.

Inside the submarine the Captain took a last look through the periscope.

'Funny!' he said. 'I can't see a thing. There seems to be something blocking it.'

'Let's have a look,' said the First Officer.

'Good heavens! The Admiral's moggy! We'll have to surface.'

'Moggy?' the Captain said. 'What is a . . . ?'

'Cat,' said the First Officer. 'You remember; the one that inspected us. I thought he would have taken her ashore with him. Careless chap. Oh well. Surface?'

'Yes,' sighed the Captain. 'Someone will have to take her ashore.'

So Suzy found herself slowly rising as the ship came to the top of the water again. It *was* a relief! But what were they up to? It really was a most peculiar ship, sinking and un-sinking itself like this. Suzy didn't like it at all.

So she wasn't too upset when a sailor picked her off the conning-tower and took her into a rubber dinghy. It had an outboard motor and they were soon back at the quay.

Suzy had leapt out and was nearly halfway back to Auntie Jo's house before the sailor had had time to secure the dinghy to the harbour wall.

'I was afraid you were lost at sea,' said Auntie Jo when Suzy walked in. 'I nearly cried in Church when we sang a hymn about "those in peril on the sea".' She sang the last bit in a quavery voice. Biff sang it after her in an even more quavery voice.

'For those in peril on the sea. Clever Biff.'

'Oh you are a clever Biff,' said Auntie Jo.

'On the sea. On the sea. Clever Biff. On the sea.' Biff liked singing.

Auntie Jo put a saucer down for Suzy, who had nearly been in peril *under* the sea. It was chicken giblets. It wasn't fish, but it was very good. Suzy ate it all up.

'Merci,' she said, cleaning her whiskers.

'You have got a funny miaow,' Auntie Jo said.

'Merci,' said Biff, and then he began to sing. 'On the sea. On the sea. Clever Biff. On the sea.'

Auntie Jo and Suzy were just a little tired of that hymn by bed-time.

Before she went upstairs, Auntie Jo stroked Suzy 'good night'.

Suzy purred.

But she did miss Gaby stroking her the wrong way.

7   *Home by car?*

The next morning Auntie Jo got out her tricycle as usual. Suzy popped into the basket, but then jumped out again and went back into the house. She felt that she ought to say goodbye to Biff because she was *sure* that she would get home to France today.

'Au revoir,' she said, which is French for 'goodbye'.

Biff cocked his head to one side.

'Clever Biff!' said Biff. 'Hello, Auntie Jo.'

Suzy felt that he hadn't got it quite right. When you say goodbye to somebody they usually say goodbye back to you. So she tried again.

'Au revoir.'

This time Biff got it. 'Au revoir!' he said. 'Clever Biff. Au revoir.'

Suzy ran out and was only just in time to catch Auntie Jo, who was already out of the gate.

'I thought you had decided not to come today,' Auntie Jo said as she stopped for Suzy to hop in.

'Chez-moi,' said Suzy.

'You have got a funny miaow,' Auntie Jo said.

They pedalled off down to the shops on the sea-front. Auntie Jo parked the tricycle outside the baker's shop. As she got down from the saddle she turned to Suzy who was poised to jump out of the basket.

'I wonder where you are off to this time?' she said. 'Well, I suppose we will see you at supper,' and she went into the baker's shop.

Suzy jumped down and hurried across the road. She had just spotted something familiar on the other side. It was a French sailor with a bobble on his cap! A French sailor might lead her to a French ship. Suzy began to follow him along the pavement.

The sailor was walking very fast; Suzy had to keep running to keep up with him. They seemed to be going a very long way. After a while the pavement became more crowded and the traffic going past them got heavier and noisier. Suzy realized that they were coming to a big port. She could see cranes and wharves and the masts and funnels of ships.

Ships! Suzy kept as close to her sailor as she could. Oh, surely he would lead her to a French ship!

Poor Suzy. He didn't lead her to a French ship. She lost him altogether for he turned into a large building and disappeared. Suzy tried to follow him, but there was a swing door, and when she tried to go through, it just swung her right round and back on to the step again! She tried again and the same thing happened.

Oh, well. She didn't need the sailor now. He had led her to a port. One of those ships *must* be going to France.

Suzy trotted along a wide road towards the quays where the ships were. There were lots of cars going the same way. One of them drew up at the kerb near Suzy and the driver called out to a man in uniform.

'Is this the way for the ferry to France?'

'That's right, sir. Just keep straight ahead,' said the man.

France! Suzy must stay with this car. As the car moved off again she began to run. It was much harder than following the sailor – Suzy ran and ran until her paws ached.

She was almost giving up when the car slowed to a halt. There was a queue of cars waiting to board the ferry. Suzy had not expected to go home to France by car, but it looked as if that was what she was going to have to do. She ran along the queue looking for a car that she could get inside without being noticed.

She found the very one. The family it belonged to had brought so much luggage that the boot would not shut properly and was tied half-open with rope. This left room for Suzy to nose her way in between a suit-case and a deckchair and find a nice little space where she could curl up. The family in the car behind might have noticed her, but luckily they were busy looking at a map of France to see where they would have to go when they got to the other side of the Channel.

Suzy's car moved slowly forwards. Sud-denly there was a great clanking as they went down the ramp and into the hold of the ship. It was dark down there, but there were some lights on. Suzy kept very still, a bit frightened by all the banging and clanging as people got out and slammed their car doors. There were cars behind and cars in front and cars on each side. The slams echoed round the metal sides of the ship.

Suzy's family got out of the car and disappeared through a little door in the side where everybody else was going.

At last it was quiet. Suzy peeped out. There was nobody about. She squeezed between a couple of cars and made for the door that her family had gone through.

But there was a new noise. Suzy stopped and listened. It was the ship's engines. They were off!

Suzy hurried on up some steep stairs and came out into a corridor. This led into a big room full of people sitting at tables and eating. Suzy thought it was a very funny ship – more like a house. Then she saw some more stairs. Could there be bedrooms up there? Suzy climbed up and came out on deck into the sunlight.

There was sea all around them. Suzy ran to the rail that went round the side of the ship and then along it to the stern at the back. She could see England disappearing behind them!

She ran down the other side to the very front of the ship, the bows, and found herself a piece of curled-up rope to sit on.

Suzy sat there, her eyes set towards France.

She was going home at last.

8   Home at last

There was Suzy, sitting like a figure-head in the bows of the ship, getting nearer to France every minute.

A little girl came and sat with her. 'Are you the ship's cat?' she asked.

'Chez-moi!' said Suzy.

'You do have a funny miaow,' said the little girl. 'Granny, look. I've found the ship's cat, and she's got such a funny miaow. You listen.'

Suzy didn't say anything else. She had explained where she was going.

'Perhaps she'd like a bit of sardine sandwich,' Granny said.

Suzy did like it. She ate it all up and cleaned her whiskers.

'Merci,' she said.

'I told you she'd got a funny miaow,' the little girl said to her granny.

Lots of other children came and talked to Suzy, but she didn't move from her position in the bows, which was the nearest she could get to France.

It seemed a very long time, but at last a thin line of land appeared ahead of them.

'Look! Look! There's France!' the little girl shouted, pointing.

France! Suzy could hardly believe it. Soon she would be home.

Just then a sailor came along – and he saw Suzy.

'What's that cat doing there?' he said.

'It's the ship's cat,' said the little girl. 'Didn't you know?'

'No, I didn't,' the sailor said. 'We haven't got a ship's cat. She's a stowaway.'

He reached forward and made a grab at Suzy. Suzy dodged him. He didn't look friendly at all. He wasn't.

He chased her all around the ship – down the stairs, along corridors, through the dining-room, past the shop and back up on deck again.

Soon all the children began to join in. They thought it was a wonderful game.

Poor Suzy. She was so near home. Nothing must stop her now. She must hide, but where? Anyway, the mob of laughing, shouting children was too close behind her.

Then she saw the mast. She ran up it like

72

a squirrel and clung at the very top. Everyone stopped and looked up. No one could reach her.

'I'll get her down,' said the puffing sailor. He went off to fetch a ladder.

Suzy stared around her desperately. There was France getting nearer and nearer – France and home.

Then she saw something else. In the sea ahead of them was a French fishing boat.

And on the deck were four little boys like steps.

It was Suzy's family! It must be.

'Out of the way there!' said the sailor, clearing the children from the foot of the mast. He had come back with a ladder.

But Suzy didn't notice. She leapt straight over his head on to the deck, ran to the rail – and dived!

'Oooooh!' said everybody watching.

'She'll drown!' cried the little girl. 'Somebody save her! Quick!'

But Suzy didn't drown. She seemed to go a very, very long way down into the green water, and then she paddled hard with her little paws and came up to the surface like a cork.

She began to swim. The ship's side towered above her, with a row of faces along the rail. Suzy couldn't see the fishing boat any more because of the waves, but she swam towards the place where she had seen it last.

The little girl waved her arms madly at the boys on the fishing boat and pointed down to Suzy.

'Cat overboard!' she shouted.

The other children joined her: 'Cat overboard!'

The little French boys did not understand, but they saw that the children were pointing to something in the sea. They got their father to turn towards it.

At last there was a calm stretch of water between two waves and the boys spotted something moving there. In a few seconds Suzy was scooped out of the sea with a bucket.

The ferry was already some way away, but they could hear the children cheering because Suzy was safe, and see them waving goodbye.

Suzy was more than safe – she was very, very happy. She sat there in the bucket purring like a ship's engine.

'It's a cat!' said Pierre. 'A swimming cat!'

'Stripey,' said Henri.

'With football socks,' said Paul.

'It's Suzy!' said Gaby, lifting her tenderly out of the bucket and holding her close. 'I knew she would come back.'

That evening, in England, Auntie Jo was getting worried. No Suzy.

'I wonder where she is?' she said aloud. 'She's never missed her dinner before.'

'Shocker!' said Biff. 'Hello, Auntie Jo. Au revoir!'

'What did you say?' Auntie Jo said.

'Clever Biff. Au revoir. Au revoir.'

'Now where did you learn that?' said Auntie Jo. 'I've not taught you that. Of course, she did have a funny miaow. I wonder. . . .'

And the French cat that Auntie Jo was wondering about? She was so full of fish that she could hardly move. She was on the rug in the boys' bedroom in France, being watched by four pairs of shining eyes. She was purring and purring as though she would never stop. Gaby was stroking her the wrong way!

Suzy was home at last.

You can see more Magnet Books on
the next page.

For a full list of Magnet titles, please write to:

Magnet Books,
Cash Sales Department,
PO Box 11,
Falmouth,
Cornwall TR10 109EN

Also by Jill Tomlinson
in Magnet Books:

The Gorilla Who Wanted to Grow Up

Pongo is a young gorilla who longs to grow
up. He has long glossy black hair but
cannot wait till he grows a silver back, and a
big chest that he can thump – just like his
father. Each of his adventures, often with
his new baby sister, makes him a little more
grown up.

Illustrated by Joanne Cole

The Hen Who Wouldn't Give Up

Hilda the Hen's Auntie has just had a new family
of chicks and Hilda would like to visit them, but
it's too far to walk, so she decides to get a lift.
That's not as easy as she thinks and she has some
quite startling adventures on the way. But Hilda
is brave and determined, and her persistence
wins through in the end.

Illustrated by Joanne Cole

Penguin's Progress

Otto, being the first penguin chick of the year, has the bewildering task of bringing up all the younger ones. He doesn't know where to start, and the grown-up penguins are far too busy to explain. So he just has to watch what they do and try to copy them, until in the end he learns how to swim, dive and catch his own fish.

Illustrated by Joanne Cole